To Caleb, Eli, and Alec

You are my inspiration and my motivation.
I love you beyond limits.
I know you will do great things.

# I HAVE A NAME

## Speak Kindly

No Bullying Allowed

phie

Liang

Brayton

Saanvi

Aamira

Written by

## Ms. Fancy Pants Running Dance
## Sparkle Star Lovely - That's Me

Level Up
3 & 4
Readers

Character Illustrations by

## Ishika Sharma

## Physical Bullying

Hitting

Biting

Kicking

## Cyberbullying

## Verbal Bullying

Bullying is...

Name - Calling

Spreading Rumors

Punching

Sharing harmful Message

Sending harmful Message

Posting harmful messages

# I Have a Name

## Speak Kindly

Sophie

Aamira

Brayton

Saanvi

Liang

Clickety-clack. Thumpity-thump. The sound of children playing. Sophie, Aamira, Saanvi, Brayton, and Liang played together in fun harmony. Smiling, and laughing and happy as can be.

One day Sophie had an idea to set out on an adventure to travel the world and make new friends. Sophie wondered if her friends would join her.

Anxious to find out, Sophie shouted in excitement. "I have an idea," said Sophie. "Let's visit new places and make new friends."

"That sounds great," Liang said. "Can I come too?" asked Saanvi.

"Skippity dippity doo. I love you. We can all go." Sophie screeched as she shuffled her feet and wiggled her arms.

Away they went. Traveling the United States and across the world. On a mission to new continents, and new countries.

As they set out on their journey, the kids decided to call themselves, "The Traveling Five," and they created what they called the traveling song.

# 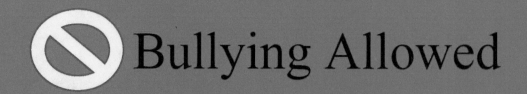Bullying Allowed

Just then, Sophie started the traveling song with a rap.

On our way to make new friends. On our way to see new lands. We are going to change the world. I am going to shake and twirl. Be kind and don't you fight. I am bringing joy and light.

Please don't call me ugly. Please don't call me fat. Please don't call me cranky; My mom didn't name me that.

I am beautiful and I am smart. Sing this song and sing this rhyme. I have a name so please be kind. No Bullying allowed. No bullying allowed.

I am nice and I am proud. I am here to rock this crowd. No bullying allowed. No bullying allowed.

# I HAVE A NAME

## Speak Kindly

Shrieking with excitement, Brayton burst into song. "Diddle widdle deedle doo. Through the lands we follow you. The Traveling Five is what we are. Under the moon and through the stars."

"Hip hip hooray. We had a funtastic day." Saanvi squealed and swirled all around. The Traveling Five made many friends and great memories along the way.

But no matter where they went, they always met a few that did not act very cool.

"We traveled the world giving love though not everyone was kind." Saanvi whispered as she shrugged her shoulders.

Then something unfortunate happened. The Traveling Five met some not so nice people shouting some not so kind words.

"You look funny."

"I don't like you."

"Get out." "Leave."

"You don't belong here."

As the angry clouds filled the air, the mean words brought sadness to those around them.

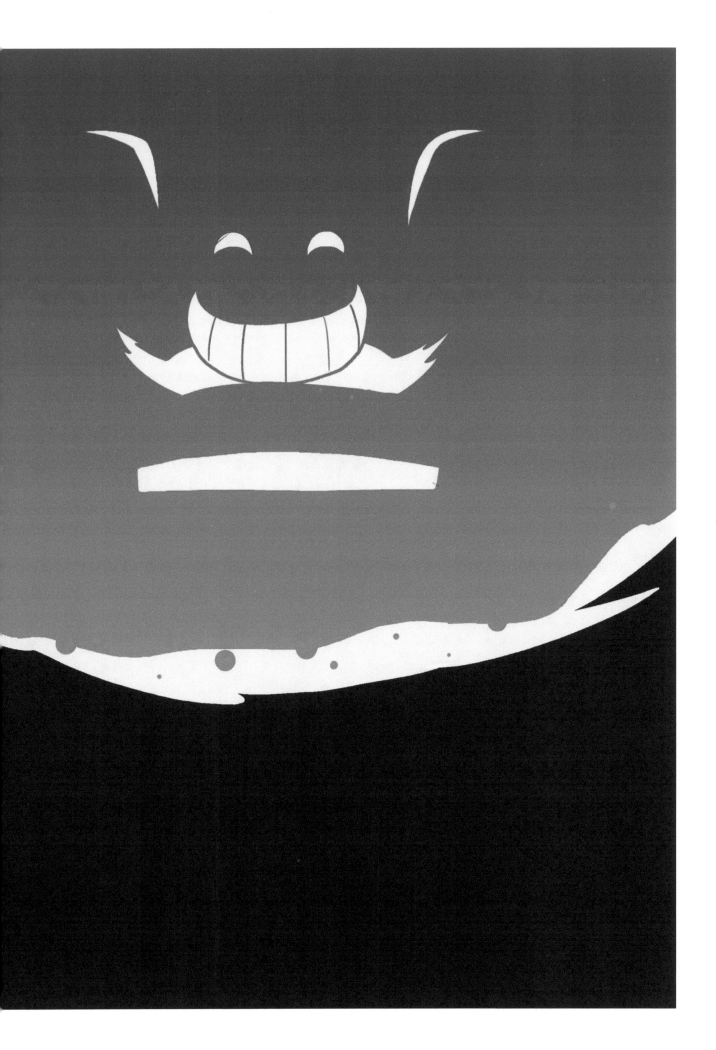

Sophie began to feel bad about herself as the clouds swirled her head.

"I don't feel good," said Sophie. "I don't know what to do."

"Oh no, the mean words are making Sophie sad," said Aamira.

"We have to help Sophie," screamed Liang. Determined to help their friend, the travelers told Sophie the things they loved about her.

Just then, Sophie gained her superpower. She started to believe all the things her friends were saying.

Sophie screamed, "I am amazing! I am great! I am enough!"

Sophie kept repeating the words. "I have a name. Speak kindly. I have a name. Speak kindly." Brightness filled the land, and the clouds began to disappear.

Saanvi started to see the light too. "Yippy yay! The darkness is going away." Saanvi shouted as she did her happy dance.

But some people still did not understand. They slammed the door in Aamira's face.

Saddened over what happened, Aamira begins to sing. "Traveling the world is where I've been. Please don't shut me out. Just let me in. I just want to be your friend. No bullying allowed."

"Some people don't want us to be happy. Why is this happening?" Brayton asked.

"They are fighting us like the waves in the ocean. We just want to be your friend. I have a name. Speak kindly. No bullying allowed."

"Oh no! The mean words are back. Don't listen. We must fight it with kindness. We can do it. We can make the mean words go away!" Brayton yelled as he ran toward his friends.

"Use your superpower," Sophie screamed. "Don't let the darkness in. Scream kind words. It will make the mean words go away."

Just then, The Traveling Five started to yell.

We are beautiful

We are kind

We are smart

We are love

**We are enough! No Bullying Allowed!**

# I Have a Name. Speak Kindly

Words have power. People deserve to feel safe. No hitting. No punching. No teasing. No name-calling.

## No Bullying Allowed

ESTONIA
LATVIA
LITHUANIA
AND
BELORUSSIA
RUSSIA
UKRAINE
MOLDAVIA
OMANIA
LGARIA

The Traveling Five
Kids Can Change the World

# Take the Pledge
 Bullying Allowed

## I Promise to **STOP** Bullying

I promise to be kind and respectful to everyone including myself.

I promise not to hit, punch, slap, kick, bite, or physically hurt myself or anyone else.

I promise not to call anyone mean names.

I promise to speak up and tell an adult if I feel bullied.

I promise to include everyone and be a great friend.

I promise not to tease anyone.

I promise not to lie or spread rumors.

I promise to tell an adult if I see anyone getting bullied.

I promise not to post, share, or send harmful messages using the phone, computer, or tablet.

Signed:

| I Have a Name. Speak Kindly. No Bullying Allowed. | Name: _____ |
| | Date: _____ |
| | Grade: _____ |

## Draw a No Bullying Sign

| | |
|---|---|
| I Have a Name. Speak Kindly. No Bullying Allowed. | Name: _____ <br> Date: _____ <br> Grade: _____ |

## Name Three Ways You Will STOP Bullying

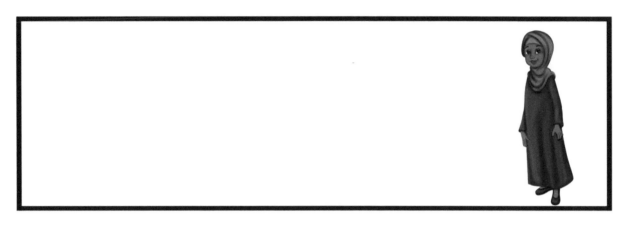

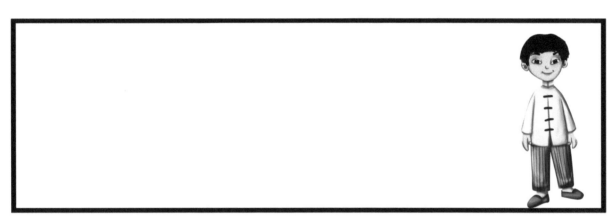

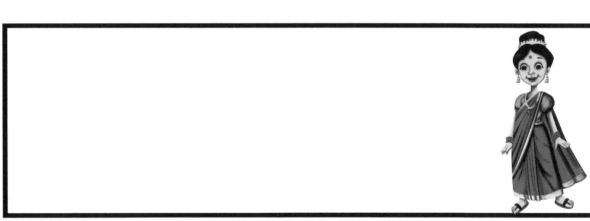

| I Have a Name. Speak Kindly. No Bullying Allowed. | Name: _____ |
| | Date: _____ |
| | Grade: _____ |

If you are being bullied, or if you see someone being bullied.

## WHAT SHOULD YOU DO?

_____

_____

_____

_____

_____

_____

_____

_____

_____

_____

_____

_____

_____

_____

_____

_____

_____

# I Have a Name. Speak Kindly. No Bullying Allowed.

## Write Your No Bullying Story

# What do these words mean to you?

### Write the definition and then discuss with an adult

Acceptance

Anti-Bullying

Cyber Kindness

Dignity

Friendly

Inclusion

Kindness

Polite

Respect

Support

# GREAT JOB!

Read other important messages from National Worldwide Syndication.
Available on Amazon and Barnes & Noble.

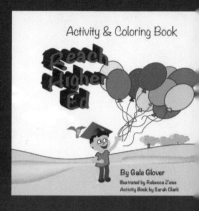

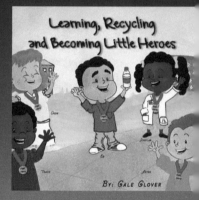

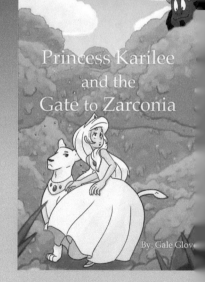

CPSIA information can be obtained
at www.ICGtesting.com
Printed in the USA
BVHW022157120522
636949BV00004B/11